This book belongs to :

Tall Tale Tom

Text © Anne Forsyth 1994

Illustrations © Val Biro 1994

First published in Great Britain in 1994 by

Macdonald Young Books

大話湯姆

Anne Forsyth　著

Val Biro　繪

刊欣媒體營造工作室　譯

三民書局

Chapter One

"**W**ell, I don't **believe** a word of it," said the gray cat.

"Please yourself," said Tom, the black and white cat.

The other cats sat around, their eyes like **saucers** in the light from the street lamp.

"What an **amazing** story!" said the little ginger cat. She thought Tom was wonderful.

第一章

「哼！我一點兒都不相信！」灰貓說。

「信不信隨你囉！」黑白貓湯姆說。

其他的貓圍坐一旁。他們瞪大的眼睛在街燈下就像發亮的托盤。

「好神奇的故事喲！」黃褐色的小貓說。她覺得湯姆好棒喔！

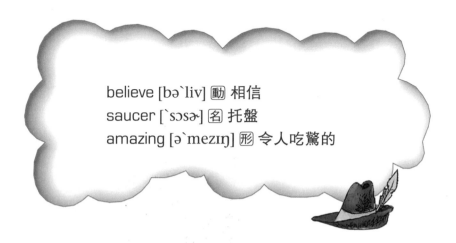

believe [bə`liv] 動 相信
saucer [`sɔsɚ] 名 托盤
amazing [ə`mezɪŋ] 形 令人吃驚的

He told such tales of his **adventures**. How he'd flown over the North Pole, then landed on an **iceberg** and made friends with the polar bears.

How he'd **saved** a beautiful **princess** and she had given him a golden **collar**.

"Where is it then?" said Smudge, the gray cat.

湯姆說了許多他的冒險故事，說他如何飛到北極，然後降落在一座冰山上，而且還和北極熊交朋友。

　　說他如何拯救一位美麗的公主，公主還送給他一個金項圈。

　　「那項圈呢？」灰貓史墨基問。

adventure [əd`vɛntʃɚ] 名 冒險
iceberg [`aɪsˌbɝg] 名 冰山
save [sev] 動 拯救
princess [`prɪnsɪs] 名 公主
collar [`kɑlɚ] 名 項圈

Tom loved **making up** stories. Ever since he was a kitten, he'd told **tall** stories — stories with himself as **hero**. You would never have known to look at him. He was black and white. He looked just like any old cat. There were dozens like him **wandering** about the town, hunting or **scrounging** in the dustbins.

But Tom was different. For one thing, he didn't have a home. Sometimes, he sat outside the back door of the butcher's shop, hoping for **scraps**. Sometimes he slept under the bushes in the park. Most of the time, he lay in the sun, making up stories.

湯姆最愛編故事了。當他還是一隻小貓的時候，他就喜歡講一些誇張的故事，把自己說成故事裡的英雄。仔細瞧他，你很難想像呢！他只是一隻黑白花貓，跟普通的貓兒沒兩樣。像他一樣在街頭上晃蕩，在垃圾桶裡翻找食物的貓多得是。

　　可是湯姆有一點不同，他沒有個家。有時候，他坐在肉舖的後門外頭，希望能分到一點剩菜剩飯；有時候，他睡在公園的樹叢底下。大部分的時間他就躺在太陽底下，編著故事。

make up　捏造
tall [tɔl] 圏 誇大的
hero [`hɪro] 图 英雄
wander [`wɑndɚ] 勔 徘徊，漂泊《about》
scrounge [skraʊndʒ] 勔 四處搜尋
scrap [skræp] 图 剩飯

⑦

Of course, everyone knew that the stories weren't true. But wasn't it great that Tom could **invent** such tales!

"Stories!" **sniffed** Smudge. "Why can't you get a proper job like everyone else? Look at Toby — he works at the **fish and chip** shop. Look at Tibs — she helps at the school. If you *could* get a proper job, which I **doubt**."

Tom was very **annoyed** by this. "'Course I could get a job," he said. "Give me a day or two."

He thought hard about it. He had to have a special job. Something exciting and adventurous.

當然，大夥兒都知道這些故事是假的。可是湯姆能想出這麼些故事，也真是不簡單。

「又在編故事了！」史墨基不屑地說，「你就不能像其他人一樣，找份正當的工作嗎？看看陶比——他在炸魚加薯條的速食店工作；看看提比絲——她在學校幫忙。我真懷疑你能不能找到一份正當的工作。」

湯姆對此很不高興。「我當然可以找到工作，」他說，「給我一、兩天的時間。」

他努力地想著這件事。他得要有份很特別的工作，既刺激又有冒險性的。

invent [ɪn`vɛnt] 勔 虛構，捏造
sniff [snɪf] 勔 吸吸鼻子（表示輕蔑、不相信）
fish and chip 炸魚加薯條（英國典型的速食）
doubt [daʊt] 勔 懷疑
annoyed [ə`nɔɪd] 形 感到生氣的

Next day, Smudge met him by the **harbor**, **sauntering** along the **quay**.

"Hello, Tom, you got a job yet?"

"Who, me?" Tom woke up with a start. He had been making up a story about **pirates** and how he became a pirate cat.

"Oh yes," he said **mysteriously**, "I won't be around for a bit. I'm off to sea. Yo, ho, ho ...." he added.

隔天，史墨基在碼頭散步，遇到了湯姆。

　　「哈囉！湯姆，你找到工作了沒呀？」

　　「誰？我嗎？」湯姆一副大夢初醒的樣子。他剛剛編了一個關於海盜，而他如何變成了一隻海盜貓的故事。

　　「喔！對了，」他神祕兮兮地說。「我不會閒晃太久囉！我要出海去了，嘿——嘿——嘿……」他補充說明。

harbor [`hɑrbɚ] 图 港口
saunter [`sɔntɚ] 勔 蹓躂，散步
quay [ki] 图 碼頭
pirate [`paɪrət] 图 海盜
mysteriously [mɪs`tɪrɪəslɪ] 副 神祕地

"A sea cat?" said Smudge.

"That's right," said Tom. He had only thought of it that very minute. "I'm going to sea."

The more he thought about it, the more he liked the idea. Fresh air, adventure, and best of all, fish on the menu every day. He waved goodbye to Smudge and **trotted** off as fast as his paws would take him.

The first boat he saw was the *Daisy Belle*, a fishing boat that sailed up the coast fishing for herring and cod. The **captain** and his **mate** were busy **swabbing** the deck and loading fish boxes.

Tom sniffed the air. "There's a funny-looking cat on the quay," said the mate, glancing up from his work. He liked animals and had a cat of his own at home.

"Don't **encourage** it," said the captain, who wasn't nearly as fond of cats.

But Tom paid no **attention**. He liked the look of the friendly mate, so he decided then and there, that he would sail on the *Daisy Belle*. So he **hung around** the harbor until night time.

「一隻航海貓？」史墨基說。

「沒錯！」湯姆說，他不過是剛閃過這個念頭。「我要出海了！」

他愈想愈喜歡這個主意。新鮮的空氣、冒險的旅程，最棒的是，每天都有魚可吃。他向史墨基揮手道再見，飛快地跑開了。

湯姆看到的第一艘船是「美雛菊號」，這是一艘出海捕鯡魚和鱈魚的漁船，船長和大副正忙著擦洗甲板，把魚箱搬上船。

trot [trɑt] 動 快步，小跑步
captain [`kæptən] 名 船長
mate [met] 名 大副
swab [swɑb] 動 用抹布或拖把擦洗

湯姆嗅一嗅空氣。「碼頭上有一隻看起來好好玩的貓吧！」一名船員從工作中抬起頭來，瞄了一眼說。他喜歡動物，而且家裡也養了一隻貓。

「別招惹他。」不太喜歡貓的船長說。

不過，湯姆沒注意到這一點，他喜歡這個親切船員的樣子，所以他決定無論如何都要跟著「美雛菊號」出海。於是，湯姆就在港口閒蕩到晚上。

encourage [ɪn`kɝɪdʒ] 勔 鼓勵，唆使
attention [ə`tɛnʃən] 名 注意
hang around 閒蕩，徘徊

Then he made his way back to the *Daisy Belle*. She was all ready to sail on the morning **tide**.

Tom jumped and landed softly on all four paws, right on the deck.

He **curled up** behind the fish boxes and was soon fast asleep.

When he woke, he could hear a strange sound. Chug, chug, chug. The harbor wall seemed to be moving. "No, it's the boat that's moving," he said to himself. "We're off!" The sound was the **engine**.

He curled up again. "How **calm** the sea is! This is the life for me, and no mistake."

But before long, the *Daisy Belle* sailed out of the harbor and reached the open sea. The little boat began to **roll**. She rose and fell, **surging** up and down over the huge white-crested waves.

"She's **tossing** a bit," said Tom to himself.

He was rather proud of knowing that boats are always called 'she', not 'it'. "I must remember that," he thought. "Because after all, I *am* a **seagoing** cat...."

Just then, the mate noticed something moving behind the **stack** of fish boxes. "What on earth!" he said. "Well, would you look at this!"

"It's that cat," he called to the captain. "The one we saw on the quay."

然後他走向了「美雛菊號」。船已經準備好要藉著黎明的潮汐出航。

　　湯姆一跳，四腳輕輕地著地，恰好落在甲板上。

　　他蜷縮著身子躲在魚箱後面，不一會兒就睡著了。

　　醒來的時候，他聽到一種奇怪的聲音，恰——恰——恰——，港口的牆壁好像在移動。「不對，是船在動吧！」湯姆自言自語。「出發了！」這聲音原來是引擎聲。

　　他又縮起了身子，「多麼寧靜的大海呀！這是屬於我的生活，不會錯的！」

tide [taɪd] 名 潮汐
curl up　把身體蜷曲
engine [`ɛndʒən] 名 引擎
calm [kɑm] 形 平靜的

不久之後，「美雛菊號」航離了港口，來到遼闊的大海。這艘小船開始左右搖晃了起來，隨著洶湧的波濤起伏，越過白色羽冠般的巨浪。

「她搖晃得有點兒厲害呢！」湯姆自言自語地說。

其實，他對自己知道「船」要代稱為「她」而不是「它」感到十分得意。「我得記清楚這個，」他想。「畢竟我是一隻以航海為業的貓啊！」

就在這時候，船員注意到堆積的魚箱後面有個東西動來動去。「搞什麼啊？」他說。「喂！你快過來看！」

「是那隻貓吧！」他大聲叫船長。「我們在碼頭上看到的那隻貓。」

roll [rol] 動 左右搖晃
surge [sɝdʒ] 動 波濤洶湧
toss [tɔs] 動 上下搖動
seagoing [`si‚goɪŋ] 形 以航海為業的
stack [stæk] 名 堆

"**A** stowaway!" said the captain. "Well, he'll just need to stay on board till we get back."

All night long, the boat **heaved** up and down, and Tom with it. All night long, he lay and **groaned**. He felt very ill indeed. Early in the morning, the men pulled in the nets full of fish, while the **gulls screeched** overhead. But Tom paid no attention.

"**I**'ve been very stupid," he said. "I wish I'd never thought of being a seagoing cat."

At last the boat **chugged** her way back into harbor. The mate threw a fish to Tom, but Tom just **shuddered** and wouldn't touch it. He still felt very **poorly**.

「這個偷渡的傢伙！」船長說。「好吧！在我們回航之前，他也只能待在船上了。」

　　整個晚上，漁船起起伏伏，湯姆也跟著忽高忽低。整晚，他躺在甲板上痛苦地呻吟著。他真的難過極了。一大清早，船員收起滿是魚兒的魚網，海鷗在頭頂上鳴叫，湯姆卻什麼也沒注意到。

stowaway [`stoə,we] 名 偷渡客
heave [hiv] 動 起伏
groan [gron] 動 呻吟
gull [gʌl] 名 海鷗
screech [skritʃ] 動 尖聲鳴叫

「我真是笨死了！」他說。「真希望我從沒想過要當一隻航海貓！」

　　船終於又噗噗——噗噗地駛回了港口，船員丟了一條魚給湯姆，可是湯姆渾身發抖，根本不想碰那條魚。他一直很不舒服。

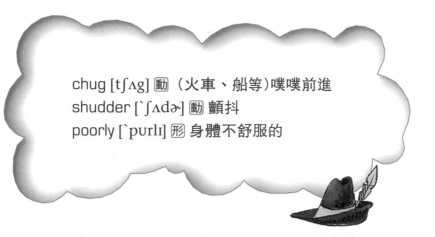

chug [tʃʌg] 勔（火車、船等）噗噗前進
shudder [ˋʃʌdɚ] 勔 顫抖
poorly [ˋpʊrlɪ] 形 身體不舒服的

As soon as he could, he jumped on to the quay. How good it was to feel dry land beneath his paws again!

"Hello, Tom!" It was Smudge, who just **happened** to be on the quay. "Are you feeling all right?" he asked.

"Me? Yes, fine!" said Tom **bravely**.

"So when are you going to sea again?" said Smudge, with a **grin**.

"Never, ever," said Tom, and hurried away as fast as he could.

Behind him, he could hear Smudge laughing.

等湯姆一覺得好些了，就迫不及待地跳到碼頭上。重新踏上陸地的感覺是多麼棒啊！

「嗨！湯姆！」是史墨基，他碰巧在碼頭上。「你還好嗎？」他問。

「我嗎？當然很好！」湯姆勇敢地說。

「那你下一次出海是什麼時候啊？」史墨基嘻皮笑臉地問。

「沒有下一次了！」湯姆邊說，邊全速狂奔而去。

他還聽到背後史墨基的笑聲。

happen [ˋhæpən] 動 偶然，碰巧
bravely [ˋbrevlɪ] 副 勇敢地
grin [grɪn] 動 咧嘴笑

Chapter Two

For a day or two Tom lay low. Then one morning, he felt strong enough to wander out and about. And of course, before very long, he **bumped into** Smudge.

"Hello," said Smudge. "Got another job yet? You *are* going to work, aren't you? Not lie around telling stories?"

"Of course," said Tom. "As a matter of fact, I've got a job," he added.

The other cats crowded round, **eager** to know what Tom was going to do next.

第二章

　　湯姆休養了一、兩天。然後有天早上，湯姆覺得自己又有力氣四處閒晃了。當然，過不了多久，他又撞見了史墨基。

　　「哈囉！」史墨基說，「找到別的工作了沒？你打算要工作了吧？不是嗎？不會到處說故事了吧？」

　　「那當然，」湯姆說。「事實上，我已經找到工作了。」他補充說明。

　　其他的貓紛紛靠攏了過來，想知道湯姆接下來要做什麼工作。

bump into... 偶然遇見…
eager [`igə] 形 渴望

"It's at the Big House," he said without thinking. The Big House was the grandest house in the whole county. It had vast gardens and a long drive that led to the house.

"Really!" Even Smudge thought this was very **splendid**.

"I'm going to be chief cat there," said Tom.

"Good for you," said the other cats.

"Bet they give you a silver dish."

"**Salmon** every day — caught by the **Duke** himself," said the little ginger cat. "You are clever, Tom."

Tom waved his paw in a **lordly** way and **strolled** down the road to the Big House.

Round the corner, out of sight of the other cats, he stopped and thought, "What *have* I said!"

Because he hadn't got a job. Not at the Big House. Not anywhere. He was making it up. He remembered his mother, Tabitha Cat, saying, "You'll get into trouble one of these days, see if you don't. Making up stories is one thing. Telling untruths is another. You will always be Found Out."

Too late! If only he'd remembered this. And now he was sure to be in trouble, because all the cats, especially Smudge, would **expect** him to be Chief Cat at the Big House.

29

「就在那棟大宅子呀！」他想都沒想就說了出口。大宅子是全鎮最華麗的房子，有廣大的花園，還有條從大門通到宅子的私人車道呢！

　　「真的啊！」連史墨基都覺得這個工作好棒喲！

　　「我要去那裡當貓總管喔！」湯姆說。

　　「你真了不起啊！」其他的貓說。

　　「他們一定會給你個銀盤子的！」

　　「每天都有鮭魚可以吃──是公爵親自抓的喲！」黃褐色的小貓說。「你好聰明喔！湯姆！」

　　於是湯姆大搖大擺地邁開腳步，悠閒地往大宅子走去。

　　走到轉角，離開他們的視線後，湯姆停下來想了一想：「我剛剛說了什麼啊？」

splendid [`splɛndɪd] 形 極好的，很棒的
salmon [`sæmən] 名 鮭魚
duke [djuk] 名 公爵
lordly [`lɔrdlɪ] 形 高傲的
stroll [strol] 動 閒逛，蹓躂

因為湯姆根本就沒有工作，不在大宅子，也不在任何地方，一切都是他編的。他想起母親泰碧莎的話：「你遲早有一天會惹上麻煩的！走著瞧吧！編故事是一回事，欺騙人家又是另外一回事，你總會被拆穿的。」

　　太遲了！要是他剛才能想起這些話就好了。這會兒，湯姆的麻煩大了！因為所有的貓，尤其是史墨基，都期待湯姆在大宅子裡當貓總管呢！

expect [ɪk`spɛkt] 動 期待

There was only one thing to do. He would have to get a job at the Big House.

He reached the great iron gates. Beyond them, the drive seemed to **stretch** for miles. He trotted along the drive until he came to the front door. Then he said to himself, "Working cats go to the back door."

He **found his way** to the back of the house, took a deep breath and **tapped** on the door with his paw.

It was opened by the cook — an angry looking woman with a red face. She looked down at Tom, and before he could say, "Have you a job for a keen, clever cat?" there was a **growl**.

32

只有一個辦法了。他得在大宅子裡找個工作。

他來到了巨大的鐵門前面，看到鐵門後面好像有幾英里那麼長的私人車道，他沿著車道走到了大門口，自言自語地說：「找工作應該到後門吧！」

他好不容易來到了後門，湯姆深呼吸一口氣，舉起腳掌輕輕地敲了門。

一位廚娘——一個樣子兇惡、滿臉通紅的女人——開了門。她低頭瞧著湯姆，湯姆還來不及說：「有沒有聰明伶俐的小貓咪可以做的工作呢？」就聽到了一聲狗叫。

stretch [strɛtʃ] 動 綿延
find one's way　好不容易才到達《to》
tap [tæp] 動 輕拍《on》
growl [graʊl] 名 （狗的）吠叫聲

33

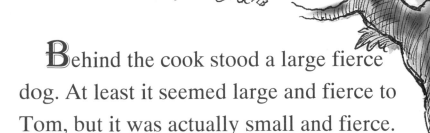

Behind the cook stood a large fierce dog. At least it seemed large and fierce to Tom, but it was actually small and fierce.

Tom didn't stop to find out. He turned and ran, **chased** by the little dog, round the house, down the drive and up into the branches of the tall oak tree by the main gate.

The little dog kept **snapping** and jumping. Tom climbed higher and higher.

After a bit, the dog got tired. It couldn't reach Tom, so turned and went back to the house.

"Whew!" said Tom. "A lucky **escape**. It should be safe to get down now."

廚娘後面站著一隻高大兇猛的狗。至少對湯姆來說，那隻狗看起來是既高大又兇猛，事實上那隻狗只能算是小又兇猛而已。

他沒停下來探個究竟，轉身就跑，那隻小狗在背後追趕著。湯姆繞過房子，沿著車道，跳到了大門旁的大橡樹上。

小狗在樹下又叫又跳，湯姆愈爬愈高。

過了一會兒，小狗累了。他抓不到湯姆，便轉身走回屋裡。

「咻──」湯姆說，「幸好逃掉了，現在下去應該安全了吧！」

chase [tʃes] 動 追趕
snap [snæp] 動 咬
escape [əˋskep] 名 逃脫

But that was the trouble.
He tried one way, then another,
but he couldn't get down.
"I'm **stuck**!" he said to
himself. "What *am* I
going to do?"

He **shivered**. "I could be
here all night — and
nothing to eat." He
peered down nervously
from the height. "Help,"
he miaowed **pathetically**.
"Help! Save me!"

At that moment, the lady of the
house drove in and stopped her car
at the gate. She **glanced** up and saw
Tom **cowering** on the topmost branch.
"Come down, **puss**, come down," she called.

"**I** can't," said poor Tom, and he **clung** on **desperately**.

"I know," said the lady. She went into the little house at the gate, and asked the lodge keeper for help. He came out with a ladder, but he still couldn't reach Tom.

但問題來了，他試試這邊，又試試另一邊，下不去呢！「我被困住了。」他自言自語地說，「怎麼辦呢？」

湯姆全身發抖，「整個晚上我都得待在這裡，也沒東西吃了。」他緊張地從這麼高的地方往下一瞄，「救命啊！」湯姆可憐兮兮地喵喵叫，「救命啊！救救我呀！」

就在這時候，大宅子的女主人開車回來了，車子就停在大門口。她抬頭看到在樹梢上縮成一團的湯姆，便叫喚著：「下來呀！小貓咪！趕快下來！」

stick [stɪk] 勔 動彈不得
（過去式、過去分詞 stuck [stʌk]）
shiver [`ʃɪvɚ] 勔 顫抖
pathetically [pə`θɛtɪklɪ] 勯 悲傷地
glance [glæns] 勔 瞥見
cower [`kauɚ] 勔 蜷縮
puss [pus]（= pussy [`pusɪ]）名 貓咪

「不行啊！」可憐的湯姆邊說，邊死命地抓著樹枝。

「我知道了！」女主人說著，便走進大門旁的小房子裡要門房幫忙。門房拿了把梯子出來，但還是構不到湯姆。

cling [klɪŋ] 動 抓住
（過去式 clung [klʌŋ]）
desperately [ˋdɛsprɪtlɪ] 副 絕望地

"**N**othing for it," said the lady of the house **briskly**. "We'll have to call the **fire brigade**."

Tom was **overcome** with shame. "Oh, dear," he said. "I am in a **mess**, and it's all my own fault. I should never have made up that story to begin with."

The **fire engine** arrived with a clanging of bells. In no time at all, the **fire fighters** had put up an extra long ladder and one of the fire fighters climbed up and **grabbed** Tom.

By now a little crowd of people had **gathered**. They all **cheered** when the fire fighter and Tom reached the ground safely.

"Is he one of ours?" asked the lady of the house.

"No, madam," said the lodge keeper. "He's an outside cat."

The fire engine drove away and all the people went back to what they'd been doing. Tom **slunk** out of the gates. He was *so* **ashamed**.

41

「這樣不行呀！」女主人果斷地說。「我們得打個電話給消防隊！」

　　湯姆羞得無地自容，「天啊！」他說，「這一切都是我的錯，惹出一堆麻煩。都怪我編出那個故事！」

　　消防車咿嗚咿嗚地來了，消防隊員立刻架上超長的梯子，其中一位消防隊員爬了上去，抱住湯姆。

briskly [`brɪsklɪ] 副 敏捷地
fire brigade 消防隊
overcome [ˌovɚ`kʌm] 動 壓倒
mess [mɛs] 名 麻煩的局勢
fire engine 消防車
fire fighter 消防隊員
grab [græb] 動 抓住

這時附近已經圍了一群人。當消防隊員和湯姆安全地下到地面時，大家全歡呼了起來。

「這是我們的貓嗎？」女主人問。

「不是的，太太。」門房說。「他是外頭的貓。」

消防車開走了，一夥兒人也各自回到工作崗位上，湯姆偷偷地從大門溜走，他覺得丟臉透了。

gather [`gæðɚ] 動 聚集
cheer [tʃɪr] 動 歡呼
slink [slɪŋk] 動 溜走
　（過去式 slunk[slʌŋk]）
ashamed [ə`ʃemd] 形 丟臉的，羞愧的

"**H**ello, Tom." It was Smudge. "**Fancy that**!" he said. "I saw you stuck up that tree. Well, that was a tall story and no mistake."

Tom paid no attention, but **made his way** along the road, his tail and whiskers drooping sadly.

What was he going to do? He had to find a new job quickly. All the other cats would be laughing at him.

「嗨！湯姆！」又是史墨基，「可真令人驚訝呀！」他說。「我看到你被困在樹上。嗯！這的確是一個很精采的故事。」

　　湯姆什麼也沒聽進去，垂頭喪氣地沿著馬路走了。

　　他該怎麼辦呢？他得儘快找份新工作，不然，其他的貓就要笑話他了。

Fancy that!　真令人驚訝！
make one's way　前進
droop [drup] 動 下垂

Chapter Three

Next day Tom was going past the village hall, feeling very low in **spirits**. Then he heard sounds from inside. There seemed to be quite a lot of noise and raised voices.

"I **wonder** what's happening in there," he said to himself and put his head round the door.

第三章

　　隔天，湯姆心情鬱悶地走過村子的大禮堂，聽到裡面傳來陣陣嘈雜的聲音。

　　「我想裡頭出了什麼事喲！」湯姆湊到門邊，自言自語地說。

spirit [`spɪrɪt] 图 心情（常用 spirits）
wonder [`wʌndɚ] 勔 對…感到好奇

"**W**e can't have actors that throw **tantrums**," said a grown-up voice. "It was a good idea, but I think the cat will have to go."

"Who, me?" said Tom. He was used to being in trouble by now.

But then he saw a small girl carrying a large gray **fluffy** cat who was **struggling** in her arms.

As the girl and the cat reached the way out, the cat said, "That's it then. I'm not going to stay where I'm not wanted. I've been in more **pantomimes** than most cats have had hot dinners. *And* I was on a calendar last Christmas but one. I won't be **bossed** around."

48

"**W**hat happened?" asked Tom.

"Call it a bit of a **dustup**," sniffed the cat. "I just don't like being bossed around. People banging tins and wanting you to run across the stage. No, thank you." He **yawned**. "So I told them. I **hissed** and **spat**."

The voice died away and the door **swung** to behind the girl and the gray cat.

But you could still hear the cat's voice. "I've been on a calendar. I told her."

49

「我們的演員可不能有這麼大的脾氣。」有人提高嗓門說。「那個主意雖然很好，不過這隻貓一定得走路。」

「誰？我嗎？」湯姆說。他現在已經習慣了這種處處惹人嫌的日子。

接下來，他看見一個小女孩走向門口，一隻毛茸茸的大灰貓在她的胳臂中掙扎著。

他們走到門口，那隻貓開口說：「夠了！我也不想待在不受歡迎的地方，我演過的童話劇比其他貓吃過的大餐還多，去年我還上了不只一本的耶誕月曆呢！我可不想在這裡被吆喝來、吆喝去的。」

tantrum [`tæntrəm] 图 （小孩的）發脾氣
fluffy [`flʌfɪ] 形 毛茸茸的
struggle [`strʌgl̩] 動 掙扎
pantomime [`pæntə,maɪm] 图 童話劇
boss [bɔs] 動 呼來喚去 《around》

「怎麼了？」湯姆問。

「算是一點小小的爭執吧！」那隻貓不屑地說，「我就是不喜歡被呼來喚去的。為什麼別人敲罐子的時候，我就得跑過舞臺？免談！」他打了個呵欠。「所以我告訴他們，我非常地不滿。」

他們身後的門啪地一聲關上了，聲音也就愈來愈小。

但隱約還聽得到那隻貓說著：「我告訴過她，我上過月曆呢！」

dustup [ˋdʌstˌʌp] 名 爭吵
yawn [jɔn] 動 打呵欠
hiss [hɪs] 動 發出噓聲表示不滿
spit [spɪt] 動 吐口水
　（過去式 spat [spæt]）
swing [swɪŋ] 動 旋轉
　（過去式 swung [swʌŋ]）

T om made his way toward the front of the hall. On the stage a boy was sitting on a log. He wore an **old-fashioned costume** and carried a long stick with a red and white spotted handkerchief tied to the end of it.

"Mrs Day," he said. "Here's another cat."

"Oh dear," said the lady **in charge**, "not another."

"It's a bit **scruffy**-looking," said the boy.

"No more cats," said the lady **firmly**.

"But you can't have a Dick Whittington pantomime without a cat," said someone else.

Tom **put on** a face that said, "Look at me. I'm very clever and handsome and **well-behaved**."

"Anyone know where he comes from?" The lady in charge looked down at Tom.

湯姆走近大禮堂的前面，看見舞臺上有一個小男孩坐在圓木上，他穿著舊式的服裝，手中長木棍的頂端還綁著一條紅底白點的手帕。

　　「黛依太太，」他說，「又來了一隻貓。」

　　「我的老天啊！」負責的那位女士說，「可別再來一次。」

old-fashioned [`old`fæʃənd] 形 舊式的
costume [`kɑstjum] 名 服裝
in charge 負責，管理

「這隻貓看起來髒ㄉㄉ的。」小男孩說。

「不准再用貓了。」黛依太太堅決地說。

「但是狄克・惠廷頓的童話劇不能沒有貓啊！」有人說。

湯姆的表情也說著：「看看我嘛！我是一隻聰明可愛又乖巧的貓喔！」

「這隻貓是從哪裡來的？」黛伊太太看著湯姆說。

scruffy [`skrʌfɪ] 形 有點髒的
firmly [`fɝmlɪ] 副 堅決地
put on 穿上，戴上
well-behaved [`wɛlbɪ`hevd] 形 行為良好的

"Looks like that cat that hangs around the butcher's," said someone.

"Well, all right," said the lady in charge. "If he's still around tomorrow night, he can be in the pantomime. Now let's get on with the **rehearsal**."

"A job!" thought Tom. "I'll **turn up** all right. I'll sleep in the hall and be as quiet as anything."

The job didn't seem to be very difficult. All he had to do was let the boy carry him on to the stage, then sit quietly while everyone else acted the play.

Later on, the lady said, "Let's see if he'll run across the stage. In the **scene** where he clears the palace of rats. Right? You hold him, Jamie, and someone bang the cat-food tin at the other side."

"Off you go, Puss." Jamie put Tom down on the stage, just as someone on the far side, out of sight, banged a tin with a spoon.

Tom ran from one side of the stage to the other. "Very good," said the lady. "Now if he can only do that tomorrow night."

Tom, cleaning the last **morsel** from the plate, raised his head and said, "You bet I can." But she didn't hear him.

「好像是常在肉舖附近閒晃的那隻貓。」有人說。

「好吧！好吧！」黛伊太太說。「如果明天晚上他還在這兒，他就可以上場。好了，我們繼續排演吧！」

「有工作了！」湯姆心想。「我要隨時待命，晚上就睡在這禮堂，而且絕不吵到任何人。」

這個工作似乎不難，湯姆只要讓那小男孩把他抱上舞臺，然後安安靜靜地坐在一旁看別人演戲就可以了。

rehearsal [rɪ`hɝsl] 名 預演，彩排
turn up 出現

不久之後，黛伊太太說：「我們來瞧瞧他會不會跑過舞臺？那個場景是貓趕走了皇宮裡的老鼠，對不對？傑米，你抱住他，另一個人躲在舞臺那邊敲貓罐頭。」

　　聽到舞臺幕後那端有人用湯匙敲著貓罐頭時，傑米放下湯姆，對他說：「小貓咪，快過去！」

　　湯姆從舞臺的這一邊跑到另一邊，「很好！」黛依太太說，「但願他明天晚上也能有這種表現！」

　　此時的湯姆已將盤子裡的貓食一掃而空，他抬起頭來說：「那有什麼問題！」不過她沒聽到。

scene [sin] 名 場景
morsel [`mɔrsl̩] 名 一口

A little later, when the rehearsal was over, he went outside. And there on the other side of the road, was Smudge.

"Hello," called Tom.

"Oh, it's you," said Smudge. "Still around? I thought you'd be off to the **jungle** or something like that."

"No time," said Tom. "I'm an actor in a pantomime."

"**Nonsense**." Smudge laughed. "I don't believe you."

"Please yourself," said Tom. "The village hall, tomorrow night. Better get there early. It's fully **booked**."

"Just another of his tall tales," thought Smudge.

But he thought he'd go along, just to see.

There was a large **poster** outside the hall.

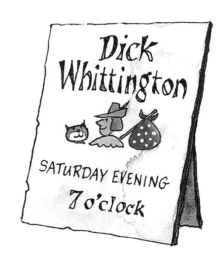

Dick
Whittington

SATURDAY EVENING
7 o'clock

彩排結束後，湯姆走到外頭，看到史墨基正好站在對街。

　　「嗨！」湯姆叫他。

　　「喔！是你啊！」史墨基說。「還在混啊？我看你還是去無業遊民的聚集處，或是諸如此類的地方吧！」

　　「才不呢！」湯姆說。「我現在是個童話劇演員喲!」

　　「鬼扯！」史墨基大笑起來。「我才不相信！」

jungle [ˋdʒʌŋgl̩] 名 失業者的集合地
nonsense [ˋnɑnsɛns] 感 瞎說

「信不信隨你。」湯姆說。「明晚兒在村子的大禮堂。可要早點到喲！位子全都被預約光了。」

　　「又在吹牛了！」史墨基心裡這麼想。

　　不過他還是認為自己該去看一看。

　　禮堂外頭的確有一張大海報。

book [bʊk] 動 預約
poster [`postɚ] 名 海報

"**I** must find out what he's up to," said Smudge.

Next evening he **crept** into the hall and found a place on the window sill. He could hide behind the curtain and **peep** through the gap, to see what was happening.

Soon people began to arrive, and before long the hall was packed. Then there was a **murmur** of excitement and the curtains **parted**.

It was warm in the hall and Smudge became **drowsy**. He hardly followed the story of the pantomime — young Dick **setting off** to seek his fortune, and then arriving at the rich **merchant**'s house.

「我要知道他到底在搞什麼花樣。」史墨基說。

隔天傍晚，他偷偷溜進禮堂，在窗檯邊找到一個位子。他躲在窗簾後面，從窗簾縫隙看過去，就可以看到舞臺上的一舉一動。

觀眾陸續進場，禮堂不久就擠滿了人。在觀眾的騷動聲中，布幕拉開了。

溫暖的禮堂讓史墨基昏昏欲睡。他幾乎不知道這齣童話劇在演什麼──年輕的狄克出發去尋找財富，到了富有的商人家裡。

creep [krip] 動 偷偷來到
（過去式 crept [krɛpt]）
peep [pip] 動 偷看
murmur [`mɝmɚ] 名 竊竊私語
part [pɑrt] 動 拉開
drowsy [`drauzɪ] 形 昏昏欲睡的
set off 出發
merchant [`mɝtʃənt] 名 商人

He grew sleepier and sleepier so he hardly heard the cook **scolding** poor Dick. He never heard Dick in his **miserable attic** room, wishing he had never left home.

But all of a sudden Smudge woke up with a start. He peered through the curtains and he could hardly believe what he saw. There on the stage was Tom.

史墨基愈來愈睏，他甚至沒聽到可憐的狄克被廚師斥責的聲音，也沒聽到狄克在簡陋的閣樓裡，希望自己從沒離開過家。

　　突然間，史墨基的精神為之一振，他幾乎不敢相信自己從窗簾後瞥見的景象——湯姆就站在舞臺上。

scold [skold] 動 斥責
miserable [`mɪzrəbl] 形 粗陋的
attic [`ætɪk] 名 閣樓

67

"Good puss," Dick was saying. "You will be my friend and help me — for I am all alone in the great city."

"Aw, isn't he lovely! Look at him." The **audience** could hardly take their eyes off Tom.

"It is — it really is him." Smudge was **astonished**.

At last, Tom, his tail held high, followed Dick off the stage. Everyone **clapped** and clapped.

Smudge was wide awake for the rest of the pantomime. Would Tom appear again?

The next act was set in the king's palace, in a strange country. And sure enough, Tom was carried on stage again.

"Who will **rid** the palace of these rats?" asked the king.

"I will." The ship's Captain stepped forward. "I have this **wonderful** animal, sent from England. Just see."

「小貓乖！」狄克說。「我一個人孤單地在這個大城市裡，也許你可以做我的朋友，在我有困難的時候幫助我。」

　　「哇！你們看，好可愛的小貓！」觀眾甚至捨不得將目光從湯姆身上移開。

　　「真──真的是他！」史墨基嚇了一大跳。

　　最後，湯姆翹著老高的尾巴，跟著狄克走下舞臺，所有的人都熱烈鼓掌。

　　史墨基可完完全全清醒了，他等著接下來的劇情。湯姆還會出現嗎？

audience [`ɔdɪəns] 名 觀眾
astonished [ə`stɑnɪʃt] 形 驚訝的
clap [klæp] 動 鼓掌

下一幕是在異鄉的國王皇宮裡。果然，湯姆又出現在舞臺上。

　　「誰能除去皇宮裡的這些老鼠呢？」國王問。

　　「我可以。」船長走向前說，「你們看，我有一隻來自英格蘭的奇妙動物。」

rid [rɪd] 勳 除去《of》
wonderful [`wʌndɚfəl] 形 奇妙的

Tom raced across the stage. He **was supposed to** be chasing the rats away. The audience couldn't see the girl at the side of the stage. She was holding a saucer of cat food and banging a tin with a spoon. The audience cheered and cheered. Tom was the **hit** of the show.

At the end all the children in the pantomime took a **bow**. So did the lady who was in charge.

Someone **presented** her with a bunch of flowers. Then the boy who played Dick **appeared**. He carried Tom — and this time Tom had a big red **bow** round his neck. All the children cheered and **stamped** their feet. Tom didn't mind the noise a bit. He knew they were cheering him.

"Such a good cat. So well behaved." The lady in charge patted Tom on the head.

湯姆跑過舞臺，應該要把所有的老鼠都趕走的。其實觀眾沒看到舞臺旁邊有個女孩，手上捧著一盤貓食，還一邊拿湯匙敲著罐頭。觀眾不停地歡呼著，湯姆成了這齣戲的大明星。

　　結束後，劇中所有的孩子及黛依太太都到臺前鞠躬。

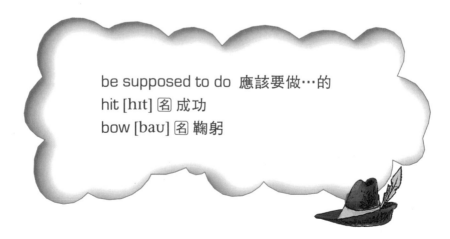

be supposed to do　應該要做…的
hit [hɪt] 名 成功
bow [baʊ] 名 鞠躬

有人送她一大把鮮花。演狄克的男孩這時候抱著湯姆走出來，湯姆的脖子上還多了一個大紅蝴蝶結。所有的孩子都興奮地踏腳叫好，湯姆一點也不覺得吵，因為他知道，這是一種讚美。

　　「這隻貓真乖、真聽話！」黛依太太摸摸湯姆的頭說。

present [prɪ`zɛnt] 動 贈送
appear [ə`pɪr] 動 出現
bow [bo] 名 蝴蝶結
stamp [stæmp] 動 踩腳

A **reporter** from the local paper wrote
all about Tom — "The **Stray** that Saved the
Show". (That wasn't quite so, but certainly Tom
had been a great **success**.)

"Where does he come from, I wonder?" said
one of the actors.

"He's often around the butcher's shop," said
another.

"But he doesn't **belong** there," said someone
else. "He's a stray."

有個當地的報社記者還把湯姆比喻為——拯救演出的流浪貓（雖然不全是這樣，不過湯姆的表現真的很成功。）

　　「奇怪？這隻貓是從哪裡來的？」有個演員說。

　　「他經常在肉舖附近出現。」另一個演員說。

　　「但他不屬於那裡。」有人說。「他是一隻流浪貓。」

reporter [rɪ`portə] 图 記者
stray [stre] 图 被遺棄的動物
success [sək`sɛs] 图 成功
belong [bə`lɔŋ] 動 屬於

"**M**rs Day," said the boy who had played Dick, "could I have him?"

"Well," the lady in charge **paused**. "You'd better ask your mum about that."

"I'd **look after** him properly," the boy **promised**. "Really I would."

"All right," Mum agreed. So they asked the butcher if they might take Tom home.

"'Course you can have him," said the butcher. "He doesn't belong anywhere."

「黛依太太，」演狄克的男孩說，「我可不可以養他？」

「嗯……」黛依太太遲疑了一下，「你最好問問你媽媽吧！」

「我一定會好好照顧他，」男孩保證，「真的！」

「好吧！」媽媽同意了。於是他們便去要求肉舖老闆讓他們帶湯姆回家。

「當然可以囉！」肉舖老闆說。「他本來就不屬於任何地方。」

pause [pɔz] 勔 猶豫，停頓
look after 照顧
promise [`pramɪs] 勔 保證

Tom was **delighted** to have a real home at last. A **cushion** to sleep on, and meals once, twice, sometimes three times a day!

"So you really were an actor," said Smudge, next time Tom appeared.

"Of course." Tom yawned. "Didn't you believe me?"

"Tell us all about it." The other cats were **longing** to hear Tom's story.

So he sat down and told them what it was like, being on the stage. "Now," he said, "you must **excuse** me. I'm going home for a sleep. Acting is very tiring."

湯姆好開心，他終於有個真正的家了。有個睡覺的軟墊子，每天吃一餐、兩餐，有時甚至三餐呢！

　　「所以你真的是個演員囉！」史墨基再度遇到湯姆時說。

　　「當然囉！」湯姆打了個呵欠。「你不相信我嗎？」

　　「告訴我們到底是怎麼一回事嘛！」其他的貓咪早就很想聽這個故事了。

　　於是湯姆坐下來，告訴他們在舞臺上表演的感覺。「好了，」他說，「請各位見諒，我得回家休息了，演戲是一件很累人的事。」

delighted [dɪ`laɪtɪd] 形 高興的
cushion [`kuʃən] 名 墊子
long [lɔŋ] 動 渴望
excuse [ɪk`skjuz] 動 原諒

"Clever Tom," said a small **tabby** cat. "What will you do next?"

"I may not be around for a little time," said Tom **airily**. "My cousin Mooncat has asked me to stay."

"I've heard of the man in the moon," said Smudge, "but never the cat in the moon."

"No?" said Tom. "Then I'll tell you all about it when I get back."

「聰明的湯姆，」一隻小斑斑貓說，「接下來你有什麼打算呢？」

　　「最近我可能不會在這附近了，」湯姆得意地說，「月球上的表哥找我去住一段時間。」

　　「我只聽說月球上有人，」史墨基說，「倒是沒聽過月球上有貓。」

　　「沒聽過嗎？」湯姆說。「好吧！等我回來以後再告訴你們。」

tabby [`tæbɪ] 名 斑紋貓
airily [`ɛrəlɪ] 副 快活地

Smudge and the other cats **stared** after him as he strolled off. It might be one of his tall tales. But with Tom, you could never be sure, could you?

They would watch out next full moon, just **in case**.

史墨基和其他的貓看著湯姆離去的背影，心裡想著，說不定又是湯姆編出來的故事；不過誰也不敢保證，它絕不會發生在湯姆身上。

　　為防萬一，他們還是注意看看下一次的月圓吧！

stare [stɛr] 動 目不轉睛地看

in case 以防萬一

每天一段奇遇、一個狂想、一則幽默的小故事
365天，讓你天天笑開懷！

中英對照喔！！

伍史利的
大日記 I、II
——哈洛森林的妙生活

Linda Hayward 著／三民書局編輯部譯

有一天，一隻叫做伍史
利的大熊來到一個叫做「哈洛
小森林」的地方，並決定要為
這森林寫一本書，這就是《伍史
利的大日記》！日記裡的每一天都有一段歷險記或溫馨有趣的小故事，不
管你從哪天開始讀，保證都會有意想不到的驚喜哦！

提昇英語能力的救星

三民英漢辭典系列

你因查不到最新的時事用語、

專有名詞或俗語而大傷腦筋嗎？

你苦於找不到有系統、

適合自己的文法書嗎？

你還在把時間浪費在電子辭典的搜尋上嗎？

三民英漢大辭典

◎ 14萬字的詞庫，幫助你在最短時間內查到你想要的字！

◎ 3萬6千個片語，幫助你最快了解英語的正確用法！

◎ 「文法概要」深入淺出，是你文法觀念的絕對救星！

三民全球英漢辭典

◎ 全書詞目超過 93,000項，釋義清晰明瞭，以樹枝狀的概念，將每個字彙分成「基本義」與「衍生義」，使讀者對字彙的理解更具整體概念。

◎ 針對詞彙內涵作深入解析，為你搭起一座通往西方文化的橋樑。

◎ 以學習者需要為出發點，將英語學習者最需要的語言資料詳實涵括在本書各項單元中。

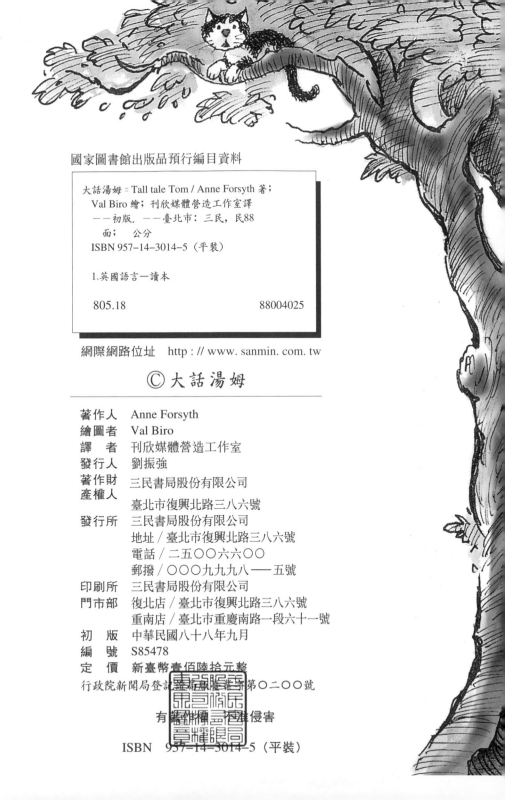

國家圖書館出版品預行編目資料

大話湯姆 = Tall tale Tom / Anne Forsyth 著；
 Val Biro 繪；刊欣媒體營造工作室譯
 ――初版. ――臺北市：三民，民88
  面； 公分
 ISBN 957-14-3014-5（平裝）

 1.英國語言―讀本

 805.18   88004025

網際網路位址　http：// www. sanmin. com. tw

著作人　Anne Forsyth
繪圖者　Val Biro
譯　者　刊欣媒體營造工作室
發行人　劉振強
著作財　三民書局股份有限公司
產權人
　　　　臺北市復興北路三八六號
發行所　三民書局股份有限公司
　　　　地址／臺北市復興北路三八六號
　　　　電話／二五〇〇六六〇〇
　　　　郵撥／〇〇〇九九九八――五號
印刷所　三民書局股份有限公司
門市部　復北店／臺北市復興北路三八六號
　　　　重南店／臺北市重慶南路一段六十一號
初　版　中華民國八十八年九月
編　號　S85478
定　價　新臺幣壹佰陸拾元整
行政院新聞局登記證局版臺業字第〇二〇〇號

有著作權　不准侵害

ISBN　957-14-3014-5（平裝）